Please Bury Me in the Library

J. Patrick Lewis

Illustrated by Kyle M. Stone

Gulliver Books
Harcourt, Inc.

Orlando Austin New York San Diego Toronto London

For Ajax and Hopper,
i nipoti splendidissimi,
With love, Grandpat
—J. P. L.

I'd like to dedicate this book to my parents, Tim and Mary Stone, for allowing me to dream, and for encouraging me to turn my dreams into goals. May every child who opens this book have parents like you.
—K. M. S.

Text copyright © 2005 by J. Patrick Lewis
Illustrations copyright © 2005 by Kyle M. Stone

www.HarcourtBooks.com

"Eating Alphabet Soup" first appeared in Michael J. Rosen's *Food Fight*, Harcourt, 1996. Reprinted with permission of the author.

"Please Bury Me in the Library" first appeared in the Fall 2000 issue of the *Journal of Children's Literature*. Reprinted with permission of the author.

Gulliver Books is a trademark of Harcourt, Inc., registered in the United States of America and/or other jurisdictions.

Library of Congress Cataloging-in-Publication Data
Lewis, J. Patrick.
Please bury me in the library/J. Patrick Lewis; illustrated by Kyle M. Stone.
p. cm.
"Gulliver Books."
1. Libraries—Juvenile poetry. 2. Libraries—Juvenile humor.
3. Children's poetry, American. [1. Libraries—Poetry.
2. Books and reading—Poetry. 3. American poetry.] I. Title.
PS3562.E9465P58 2005
811'.54—dc22 2003026983
ISBN 0-15-216387-5

K J I H G F E D C

Printed in Singapore

The illustrations in this book were done in acrylic paint and mixed media on Arches 300 lb. hotpress watercolor paper.
The display type was set in Love Letter Typewriter.
The text type was set in Ehrhardt.
Color separations by Bright Arts Ltd., Hong Kong
Printed and bound by Tien Wah Press, Singapore
This book was printed on totally chlorine-free Stora Enso Matte paper.
Production supervision by Ginger Boyer
Designed by Ivan Holmes

Contents

What If Books Had Different Names?

What if books had different names
Like *Alice in . . . Underland*?
Furious George,
Goodnight Noon,
Babar the Beaver, and
A Visit from Saint Tickle Us,
Or *Winnie-the-Pooh Pooh-Poohs,*
The Walrus and the Carp and Her,
The Emperor Has No Clues,
Or *Mary Had a Little Clam,*
And how about *Green Eggs and Spam*?
Well, surely you can think of one.
Oh, what extraordinary, merry
Huckleberry Funn!

Flea-ting Fame

Did you ever hear of the tiny book
By the famous Otto the Flea,
A fly-by-night,
Who dared to write
His Ottobiography?

Necessary Gardens

Libraries
Are
Necessary
Gardens,
Unsurpassed
At
Growing
Excitement.

Eating Alphabet Soup

My advice to the Tablespoon Slurper:

Beware what you do with that scoop!

    The Capitals, sir,

    Can cause quite a stir

In a bowlful of Alphabet Soup.

While **K, Z,** and **B** do the backstroke

Across this hot, steamy lagoon,

    The fun-loving Vowels

    May want tiny towels

To dry themselves off on the spoon.

But when Letters go swimming together

In sentences, nothing can beat

    The pleasure of reading

    The food that you're eating!

So dive in and—*bon appétit*!

Great, Good, Bad

A great book is a homing device
For navigating paradise.

A good book somehow makes you care
About the comfort of a chair.

A bad book owes to many trees
A forest of apologies.

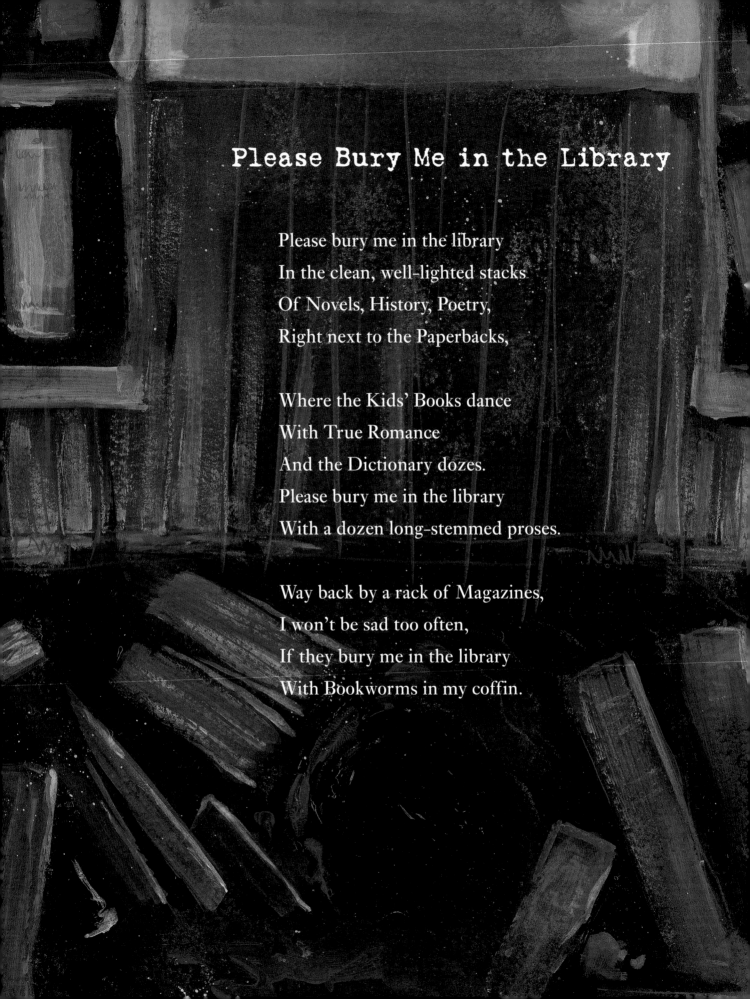

Please Bury Me in the Library

Please bury me in the library
In the clean, well-lighted stacks
Of Novels, History, Poetry,
Right next to the Paperbacks,

Where the Kids' Books dance
With True Romance
And the Dictionary dozes.
Please bury me in the library
With a dozen long-stemmed proses.

Way back by a rack of Magazines,
I won't be sad too often,
If they bury me in the library
With Bookworms in my coffin.

A Classic

A children's book is a classic
If at six, excitedly
You read it to another kid
Who just turned sixty-three.

The Big-Word Girl

Of all the clever girls I know,
     Elaine's the one who counts.
But what she counts are syllables
     In words I can't pronounce.

I took her to a horror show—
     (*Godzilla Meets Tooth Fairy*)—
But she could not unglue her eyes
     From Webster's Dictionary.

She put her trembling hand in mine
     (Godzilla smashed the floor!),
For she had come across a word
     She'd never seen before!

But when the lights came on, Elaine
     Was sound asleep and snoring.
I woke her up. She yawned and said,
     "How Uncustomarily,
       Extraordinarily,
         Incomprehensibly
          BORING!"

Reading in the Dark

I and Lantern-Eye,
my book-mad mate,
stay up late
rereading
*The Field Mouse's
Guide to Midnight,*
blinking back the
w e e   w o n d e r
of footprints,
mouse holes, and
underground maps.
"You know," I hoot
to Lantern-Eye,
"books are loaded traps."

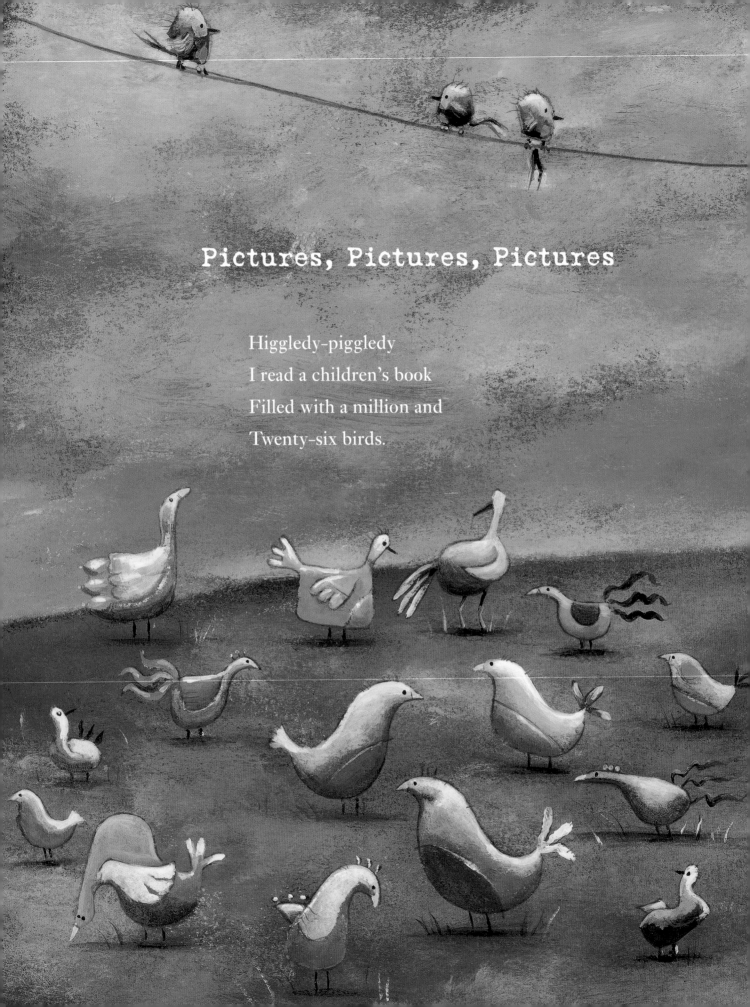

Pictures, Pictures, Pictures

Higgledy-piggledy
I read a children's book
Filled with a million and
Twenty-six birds.

Faster and *faster* and
Faster I read it be-
Cause they forgot to put
In any words!

Three Haiku

Difficult writing
Assignment: "The Story of
My Life: A Haiku"

● ● ● ●

Epitaph for a
Devoted Lifelong Reader—
Thank you for the plot

● ● ● ●

Late at night, reading
Frankenstein . . . and suddenly
a pain in the neck.

Summer Reading at the Beach

Some lay novels on their navels,

Some hold comics in their fists,

Some build castles with book shovels

From *The Times* Best-seller Lists.

Some folks read beside the ocean,

Some folks read along the coast,

Some folks rub on suntan lotion,

Some folks who forgot are TOAST!

Conversation on a Leaf

As I was reading *Caterpillars: Fascinating Fauna*,

I came across a conversation in a story on a

butterfly

who saw

her woolly

fifty-legged

relation,

and wondered,

"What's

becoming

of the younger

generation?"

The caterpillar

curlicued

to get a

better view.

"Why, Mother

dear," he

said, "I am

becoming

just

like

you."

Are You a Book Person?

A good book is a kind

Of person with a mind

Of her own,

Who lives alone,

Standing on a shelf

By herself.

She has a spine,

A heart, a soul,

And a goal—

To capture, to amuse,

To light a fire

(You're the fuse),

Or else, joyfully,

Just to be.

From beginning

To end,

Need a friend?

Ab-so-lu-tas-ti-cal

Paint me a picture book, Parrot.

Honey me poetry, Bee.

Hush me a lullaby, Owl.

Bookmark me, Flea.

Paint me and honey me, hush me right

Into an ab-so-lu-tas-ti-cal night.

Riddle me riddles, Anteater.

Pop me a pop-up, Snail.

Knit me a mystery, Black Widow.

Read deeply, Whale.

Riddle me, pop me, and knit me soon

Over the ab-so-lu-tas-ti-cal moon.

Wonder me myths, Snow Leopard.

Roar me adventures, Black Bear.

Leap me a legend, Jaguar.

Look lively, Mare.

Wonder me, roar me, and leap me high

Into the ab-so-lu-tas-ti-cal sky.

Acknowledgments

Whose book this is I hardly know,
Considering the debt I owe

To Lewis Carroll and Edward Lear.
To X. J. K.—a toast (root beer)!

To Shel and Jack, and Myra Cohn,
Who always gave this pup a bone.

To those word wizards I've left out,
The only thing to do is shout:

Whose book is this? The bottom line . . .
It's partly theirs. It's partly mine.